Secrets of the Forest

15 BEDTIME STORIES INSPIRED BY NATURE

NEON SQUID

Contents

Wood frog

Gray squirrel

Badger

Monarch butterfly

Pangolin

Margay

Southern river otter

Elephant

Welcome to the Forest

Forests are amazing places. From the snowy corners of the world to the tropics, forests provide homes to all kinds of animals and plants—including a huge variety of trees. This book contains the incredible stories of a few forest species. This map shows where they live!

Reindeer

Forests cover about 30% of all the land on Earth. Roughly 80% of the world's land animals live in them.

Sun bear

Blue-spotted mudskipper

Panther chameleon

Satin bower bird

Kauri tree

Snares penguin

March 21 is the International Day of Forests. You could celebrate by visiting a nearby forest!

The Acorn Hunt

One chilly winter morning, a squirrel woke up with a rumbling in his tummy. He peeked out from his den high up in an oak tree. Snow flurries were gently falling. A cardinal streaked across the sky in a flash of brilliant red.

The squirrel's nose twitched. He caught a whiff of wood smoke in the wind. The scent reminded him of summer. He'd been feasting on blueberries when he had sniffed something new: grilled peaches. Later, he found one on the ground. It was delicious! He spent twenty minutes cleaning every last drop of peach juice off his whiskers.

Shaking off his daydream, the squirrel dashed down the tree trunk, his sharp claws gripping the bark. His feet hit the ground, then **WHEE!** He skidded on a patch of ice and landed in a chilly snowbank. Searching for food was definitely less treacherous when it was warm outside.

The squirrel took a deep breath. He sniffed again. No fruit smells today. But something else gave his nose a thrilling tickle. Was it? Could it be? Yes! He could smell acorns! His brain raced, thinking of all the acorns he'd hidden during the fall just for a day like today. A delicious feast was waiting beneath the snow. He only had to find it…

WHOOSH! Suddenly, a blue jay dived down to the forest floor. Its beak was like a bulldozer, throwing snow, leaves, and dirt into the air. The squirrel could not believe his eyes. The blue jay was about to dig up his beloved hidden acorns! But just as the blue jay reached the layer where the acorns should have been, it got a surprise. The hole was empty. Ha! The squirrel was delighted. The blue jay had found one of the holes he'd dug and covered to trick thieves. The blue jay jeered and took to the sky. He'd have to find food somewhere else.

Over pine needles and dry leaves, the squirrel continued to scamper. Using his nose to guide him, he searched for some of the acorn hidey-holes he'd made. They were scattered throughout the nearby woodlands.

The squirrel sniffed and dug, sniffed and dug. He was so focused on the ground that he paid no attention to his surroundings. He nearly ran headfirst into a chipmunk, who was carrying an acorn in her mouth. Hmm... The squirrel hoped that one wasn't one of his.

At last, the squirrel unearthed some acorns from a hiding spot in a forest clearing. But just then a broad-winged hawk spied the squirrel from the sky. **KEE-EEE!** The hawk's sharp call startled the squirrel. He dropped his acorns fast. One rolled into a tree while another collided with a vole, who squeaked in fear and dashed off.

Frantically, the squirrel searched for a hiding spot. He quickly scampered into a rabbit hole... and avoided becoming lunch for the hungry raptor. He was disappointed to have lost part of his feast. But he knew things could have been much worse if he hadn't been a quick thinker!

The squirrel's belly was still rumbling. However, his close call with the hawk made him long for the coziness of his den. He decided not to dig out the acorns he could smell that were well below the snow's surface. Instead, he quickly retrieved some of the acorns he'd hidden in the safety of the forest. He chomped down on a stash he found under a hobblebush. Then he headed for acorns he'd buried near the muddy edges of a stream.

Finally, the squirrel had eaten his fill of acorns. He slowly made his way back to his oak tree home. He was at peace as he settled into his den. He knew there were many more acorns he could find tomorrow. He just hoped he wouldn't forget any of his hiding places. But if he did, more oak trees would grow and drop their acorns for years and years to come. Warm and snuggly, the squirrel fell into a deep and dreamy sleep.

Acorn rivals

Blue jays also collect acorns and store them for the winter. One blue jay may hide as many as 5,000 nuts in a single season!

Nuts about Nuts

In the fall, squirrels collect acorns and a variety of other nuts. They hide and bury these throughout the territory where they live. As a result squirrels are known as "scatter hoarders." The place where a squirrel hides its nuts is called a cache.

Fooling nut thieves

Gray squirrels will create fake caches to fool animals who want to steal their nuts. The squirrel digs a hole, pretends to put an acorn into it, and covers up the empty hole with dirt or leaves. Then it will secretly bury the acorn in a different place. The squirrel often does this if another animal is watching it when it is creating a cache.

Trees for the future

Amazingly, gray squirrels forget the location of up to three-quarters of the acorns they bury! But it's not all bad— this means some acorns are left to grow into new oak trees. It's great news for the oak trees and for future squirrels that will rely on them for acorns!

Super sniffers

Squirrels have an excellent sense of smell. They can find acorns buried under a foot of snow! They also use their memory to remember where their caches are located.

A Chick's Life

SPLATTER! SPLAT! SPLATTER! SPLAT! Something is coming through the tree daisy forest... Is it a herd of deer? Or a troop of monkeys? No, marching through the woods are animals you might be surprised to find here—penguins!

Dozens of adult Snares penguins are heading out from their colony in the forest. They trudge along one after another on muddy trails that lead to the coast. From the back, the long single-file line looks black. But if you look at the penguins from the front, they're much whiter! Their orangey-red bills and yellow crests add pops of vibrant color to the penguin parade.

Left behind by the adults, a fluffy penguin chick seeks out some playmates. Its parents are likely gone for the day. It moves away from the twig and mud nest where it hatched a few weeks ago.

Other chicks nearby also head out from their family nests beneath the tree daisies. There's safety in numbers. Hungry birds called petrels live nearby and wouldn't hesitate to gobble up a penguin chick. It's better to be safe than sorry!

Twenty chicks gather together to form a crèche. This fluffy penguin playgroup is perfect for young birds looking to explore. While their parents are out in the ocean diving for food, the chicks can have their own fun! One uses a fallen log like a balance beam, waving its tiny flippers for balance. Another tries to walk through a puddle of mud but makes a startling discovery. Turns out, the puddle is rather deep. **OOPS!** The chick's downy white coat quickly becomes a deep shade of brown.

The members of the crèche waddle closer to the shore. Waves crash against the rocky coast. The smell of Cook's scurvy grass adds to the salty air. Suddenly, the chicks catch a glimpse of a New Zealand sea lion. It's sleeping not far from where they are. **YIKES!** They hurriedly retreat from the massive creature.

The young penguins wander whimsically for hours on end. On the side of a damp, well-worn path, they pass shrubs covered in bright yellow flowers. When the crèche members arrive back at the dense canopy above their homes, they hear something... First is a metallic **U-TICK** sound. Then a sharp **TCHIP, TCHIP**. What is making these sounds? The puzzled chicks look around before spotting the culprits. It's a pair of Snare Island fernbirds calling to each other! They are mottled brown, making them hard to spot among the branches.

In the late afternoon, the adult penguins return to their nests and chicks. Right away they call to their young, who recognize the sound of their parents' calls. Each chick quickly scurries back to its home nest. They know what time it is! Excitedly, they open their beaks as their parents regurgitate krill, fish, and squid straight into their throats. Delicious! After this tasty meal, one of the mother penguins preens her chick's feathers.

Life in the tree daisy forest follows the same pattern day after day—fun in the morning and fish in the afternoon! The young penguins roam among the woodland and rocky beaches. They also play follow-the-leader through the trees and ferns.

As spring turns into summer, the sun shines brightly and the days get longer. The Snares penguin chicks continue to grow and change. Waterproof feathers replace their soft, downy ones. When the chicks are about 11 weeks old, it's time to leave the nest for the last time.

One, two, three... they jump off the rocky coast and into the swirling sea. **SPLASH!** Down, down, down they dive, looking for food far below the surface. One day many of these penguins will return to the daisy tree forests to raise their chicks just as their parents did.

An Island to Call Home

New Zealand is home to several different kinds of penguin. The ones in this story are Snares penguins. They live on the remote Snares Islands, about 120 miles (200 km) south of New Zealand's South Island. Male Snares penguins typically arrive at the breeding grounds in August and dig out bowl-shaped nests. A few weeks later, the females lay two eggs. The penguin mom and dad take turns keeping the eggs warm until they hatch.

Tourists are not allowed to visit the Snares Islands. They can only observe the wildlife from boats offshore.

Meet the neighbors

In addition to penguins, the Snares Islands are home to a variety of birds such as shearwaters and petrels. You won't find many big animals on this island, but look closely and you can spot impressive leaf-veined slugs and leeches.

Crammed colonies

Snares penguins form large groups called colonies on the islands. These are densely packed and can contain anywhere from 50 up to 1,500 pairs of penguins! Every few years, scientists count the number of Snares penguin nests on the islands to check how they're doing.

Growing up

Snares penguins change in appearance as they get older. Penguin chicks have thick, fluffy down (rather than waterproof feathers) when they are young. It is dark brown on their backs and heads and white on their bellies. They do not yet have the yellow crests above their eyes or bright orange-red beaks. At roughly 11 weeks old, the young penguins develop feathers suitable for swimming in the ocean. These feathers are black on their back and head and bright white on the belly.

Adventures in the Cloud Forest

Howler monkeys roar. A waterfall rushes. Insects buzz. Frogs call loudly to one another. It's amazing that any animal can get a good sleep in Costa Rica's cloud forest. And yet, that's exactly what a margay has been doing all day, tucked away in the hollow of a strangler fig tree.

Just before sunset, the small wild cat heads out from its comfy snoozing spot. YAWN! While wandering along a branch in the canopy, it comes across a three-toed sloth hanging out, chewing on leaves. The margay is hungry, but it's not eager to take on a sloth.

Just then, the margay hears a small splash. Its rounded ears rotate, searching for the source of the noise. There's a pretty pink flower in the next tree over, and poking out from inside it is a red-eyed tree frog! The margay leaps swiftly from one tree to the next. Its large, furry paws land directly on the flower. But instead of catching the frog, they end up soaked from the water inside the plant! The frog makes a speedy exit, and the margay spends the next few minutes licking the water from its paws.

As the margay makes its way back toward the tree trunk, it scurries along the underside of the thin branch. It looks like it is running upside down! Its big eyes scan the earth below. Suddenly, the margay spies a rat feeding on fruit. It's time to move.

With its ankles turned outward, the margay goes headfirst down the tree into the dark of the forest. As soon as its paws touch the ground it dashes after the rat, almost invisible against the forest floor in its spotted coat. **POUNCE!** The margay catches the rat. Its first meal of the night is tasty.

Back up in the forest canopy, the margay hangs upside down
from the branch of a tree. At first, it holds on with both of its
back feet. Then, with no hesitation, it releases the grip of one
paw. The margay is a good distance above the ground, hanging by
just one foot! A puma looks up from where it is hunting, observing
the margay performing feats like an acrobat. Just then, the
margay glimpses a young boa constrictor. In an awesome move,
it catches the snake in its jaws. This cat is a fearsome predator!

After its successful hunt, the margay scans its surroundings. It sits under the large, holey leaves of a Swiss cheese plant. It waits and watches. It doesn't take long for a spider to appear... or for the margay to catch and eat it. But then the wild cat's luck changes. Another spotted cat is lurking in the shadows. This cat is no friend of the margay. It is an ocelot hoping to make a meal of it! The chase is on.

Running as fast as its legs will take it, the margay dashes across the leaf litter. Its sharp claws dig into the bark of a nearby avocado tree. The ocelot is close on its heels. The two cats zip up the tree. A keel-billed toucan that had been resting calls out in fear: **CREE! CREE!** The margay is barely a body length ahead. It has to make a split-second decision.

Should it keep running up or head to another tree? With its long tail whipping side to side, the margay sprints along the closest branch. In a flash, it leaps from one tree to another! It's enough to lose the ocelot. The other cat makes its way to the ground, dejected. It just goes to show, you have to keep your wits about you in the cloud forest. There is always something bigger that wants to eat you...

Not long after the excitement of the chase, the first rays of sunlight start to brighten the sky. This signals to the margay that it's time to head home. Resplendent quetzals take to the skies and greet the day with a chorus of **KOWEE KEOW K'LOO**. As it walks through the forest, the margay notices a capuchin monkey feeding on flowers. A brightly colored tanager flits around, collecting moss to make its globe-shaped nest. The margay finally reaches its cozy hollow, exhausted from its adventures. As it curls up for the day, the calm sounds of a gentle breeze and light rain lull it to sleep.

A Wild Cat

Margays are spotted cats similar in size to house cats. They live in forested areas ranging from Mexico to South America. The margay in this story lives in the Monteverde Cloud Forest Reserve, in Costa Rica.

Skills to pay the bills

Margays are excellent climbers and jumpers. They can leap horizontally more than 11½ ft (3.5 m) and vertically 8 ft (2.5 m). This is a great skill when trying to catch prey in the treetops. A margay's ankles can rotate super far around, which enables the cat to descend a tree headfirst. House cats can't do this!

Yellowish-brown fur with black rosettes helps margays blend into their surroundings.

Cloud forests

Cloud forests are a type of rainforest at high altitude that is often blanketed by fog and mist. They are found in parts of the Caribbean, Central and South America, eastern Africa, Southeast Asia, and New Guinea.

A rich habitat

The Monteverde Cloud Forest Reserve is home to thousands of different species. Kinkajous and coatis are among the reserve's species of mammals. Hundreds of birds and butterflies call the reserve home. See-through glass frogs and black-speckled pit vipers are some of the reserve's many amphibians and reptiles.

Despite its relatively small size, the Monteverde Cloud Forest Reserve has roughly as many tree species as the United States!

Forest cats

The margay is just one of six cat species that lives in the Monteverde Cloud Forest, along with jaguars, pumas, ocelots, jaguarundis, and oncillas. Protected reserves like the Monteverde Cloud Forest help keep these species safe from deforestation and habitat loss.

Jaguar

Puma

Margay

The Frozen Frog

It's a frigid winter's day in Alaska. An icy wind howls through the forest. A moose takes shelter beneath a stand of spruce and aspen trees. It's waiting until the wind dies down before searching for plants to eat under the snow-covered ground.

CLUCK! CLUCK! CLUCK! A willow ptarmigan sings its flight song as it wings its way to a small clearing in the forest. The stiff breeze has exposed some seeds. As the bird forages, its feathered feet serve as snowshoes. But the ptarmigan has no idea what—or who—is below the snowy surface.

Is it a snoozing snake? No. Is it a resting rabbit? No.

Beneath the forest floor is a frozen wood frog!

Is it deep,

    deep,

        deep,

            down under the soil?

No! Instead,
this chilly critter
is just inches below
the forest floor. It has
been hidden in a burrow
under the leaf litter for
several months.

The body of this amazing amphibian is hard like a stone—a stone covered in ice. Its toes don't twitch and its muscles don't move. Its heart isn't going **THUMP-BUMP, THUMP-BUMP** and it doesn't breathe. Even the lenses of its eyes are frozen. Anyone who saw this frosty frog would definitely think it was no longer alive. But don't be mistaken—this wood frog isn't dead! It just has a smart plan to survive the cold.

As the long Alaskan winter stretches on and on, brown bears snooze snug in their dens. Still the frog doesn't wake. Dozens of caribou walk directly over the wood frog's frozen burrow. **CLICK! CLACK!** The sounds of their hooves do not disturb the frog in the slightest. It doesn't hear a thing!

Gradually, winter turns to spring. The sun's rays beat
down, slowly changing the forest floor from white to brown.
PLINK! PLUNK! Water drips off the snow-covered trees.
The frozen soil surrounding the wood frog begins to thaw.
And so does our little froggy friend.

The wood frog thaws from the inside out. The ice in its body
melts. Its skin goes from crunchy and hard to damp and soft.
Its heart starts to beat again. Blood starts to race around its
body. The frog's brain wakes up. Perhaps it wonders, "What's
happening in the wide world above?"

GULP! The frog begins to breathe. After eight
months of being a frog-sicle, the wood frog
starts moving its body. It stretches its long
legs. It wiggles its toes. Its eyes open
wide. Finally, the frog pokes its head
out from the leaves it had been
hiding below.

The wood frog hops in its rush toward the nearest pond. After months of eating nothing, food is on its mind. Its sticky tongue darts out with lightning speed. **SNAP!** The frog catches insect after insect. Overhead, a flock of common redpolls take off from a nearby tree. Their red foreheads bring a blaze of color to the awakening forest.

The pond is far from quiet. Mosquitoes buzz. Arctic ground squirrels chirp and chatter. A beaver fells a nearby tree. Day and night, the frog's calls add to the symphony of sounds.

Spring turns to summer, and the wood frog feeds and frolics in its forest home. Snowshoe hares hop around amid the Arctic lupine and other colorful wildflowers.

Fall arrives in Alaska. The nights grow cooler. The days grow shorter. Aspen and birch leaves flutter to the ground. Northern wheatears and eastern yellow wagtails head south for the winter. And so the wood frog begins digging into the dirt, preparing to defy death once more. Come spring, it will pop out again, ready for another season of adventures in the Arctic.

Life in the Cold

Wood frogs live farther north than any other amphibians in North America. They can even survive in the Arctic Circle!

Growing up fast

Female wood frogs lay thousands of eggs in large clumps. The eggs hatch anytime from about a week to a month later. These tadpoles become tiny froglets by the middle to the end of the summer. Males are fully grown in a year, while it takes females two years. They often breed in the same ponds or pools where they were born.

Sugar saves the day

So how does the frog survive being frozen alive? In fall, the wood frog's liver makes a lot of a sugar called glucose. This sugary syrup enters the cells of the frog's body, preventing them from freezing—much like the antifreeze people put in cars. If the frog's cells froze, the frog would die. But only the water *between* the cells actually freezes.

Scientists in a lab observed wood frogs as they thawed. It took about 20 minutes for the ice in the frog's body to thaw.

Going down

The wood frog isn't the only creature with clever tricks for surviving the freezing conditions of Alaska. Some fish take a winter rest too. They head down to deep, still waters below the ice of lakes and rivers, where they gather in groups. Their heart rates slow down, and they don't move much at all. Like wood frogs, they become active again when the temperatures rise in the spring.

Chillin' underground

Wood frogs aren't the only animals that spend their winters underground in Alaska. Voles and lemmings create networks of tunnels that can be hundreds of feet long beneath the snow. These rodents do not sleep through the winter. Instead, they stay cozy and feast on food they collected during warmer weather.

Red-backed voles

The Honey Hunt

The moon was high in the night sky when the
sun bear woke up. He stretched and yawned. The
moonlight made the orange patch of fur on his chest
shine like the sun. Slowly the sun bear left his cozy
bed of leaves high up in the rainforest. One paw at
a time, he made his way down to the forest floor.
Sniffing, he smelled something sweet at the base of
a tree. It was a ripe mango, just waiting to be eaten.
CHOMP! The sun bear had a feeling it was going to
be a good night. Maybe he would even come across
his favorite food: honey!

As the sun bear headed toward a
stream for a drink of water, he noticed
a hole in a tree. Sometimes holes like that
were full of honey. Hmm... The thought of
honey made his mouth water. He stood
on his hind legs, then stuck his super-
long tongue into the hole in the tree.
But no luck—when he pulled his
tongue back, there was no honey.

The water in the stream was
cool and refreshing. The sun
bear couldn't help himself. He
slid into the creek. SPLASH!

After clambering back up the muddy stream bank, the wet bear rested for a while. He was daydreaming about what he would eat next when—PLUNK! A big, spiky durian fruit fell out of a nearby tree. If that fruit had landed on his head, he would have gotten an awful headache. Instead, he got a creamy treat. Talk about lucky!

Durian fruit was tasty, but it wasn't honey, so on the sun bear went. Listening to the sounds of the forest at night was one of his favorite things to do. Insects of all colors and sizes hummed, buzzed, and whirred around him. He heard a symphony of frogs calling to one another. Suddenly, there was a WHOOSH above him. It was a flying frog! This amphibian athlete parachuted from one tree to another, landing on a giant green leaf. The sun bear wished he could fly and leap like that. But the frog wasn't a great honey-hunter like he was.

The sun bear passed colorful orchids. He passed slithering snakes. There were so many cool things to see, and yet his feet were tired. He thought about heading home, but he could not stop dreaming of his favorite treat—so on he roamed. He passed a pair of young sun bears tumbling and wrestling by a huge termite mound. Normally, he'd have torn it apart in a flash, lapping up the bugs lightning-fast. But the cubs' mother gave him a look that said, "Steer clear." So the sun bear kept walking.

The sun bear stopped and sniffed. After what seemed like ages, he thought he caught a hint of honey. The smell seemed to be coming from inside a flowering bush. He pressed himself up close and darted his tongue into the tangle of branches. But instead of honey, his tongue caught some thorns. **OUCH!**

As the first streaks of sunlight started to light up the forest, the sun bear knew it was almost time to sleep. He heard the orangutan family who lived near his home starting to stir. Suddenly a **CRACCKKK** of lightning flashed, and it began to rain. The sun bear collected twigs and leaves as fast as his paws could grab them. He carried them up his tree. He was almost done building a bed— he just needed one more trip down for supplies. The rain was bucketing down now. Leaves whizzed down from the treetops.

The sun bear couldn't wait to curl up, even if his tummy was rumbling. Branches and pieces of bark bounced off his fur. Then there was a loud **CRASH** and the sun bear spun around. Much to his surprise, whipping winds had knocked a beehive out of the crook of a tree. It had fallen and landed right behind him. Honey! Heavenly honey! He crunched and chomped, licked and lapped. Finally, when every bit of honey and honeycomb was gone, he headed back up the tree and went to sleep for the day. And never had the sun bear had sweeter dreams.

Night Bears

Sun bears are the world's smallest bears. They live in the forests of Southeast Asia, from southern China to Indonesia. This story takes place on the island of Borneo.

Sun bear, moon bear

Sun bears get their name from the yellow patch on their chest, which is lighter than the rest of their fur. It is said to look like the rising (or setting) sun. Every individual sun bear's chest patch has a unique pattern, like human fingerprints. But despite their name, sun bears are nocturnal—which means they are active at night.

Everything's on the menu

A sun bear's tongue can be 8 to 10 in (20 to 25 cm) long. That's the longest of any bear! It comes in handy for getting honey out of hives and insects out of trees. Sun bears are omnivores, which means they eat both meat and plants. They eat a wide variety of foods from bees and earthworms to coconuts and durian fruit.

Bedtime

Sun bears are arboreal, meaning they live in trees. In the Malay language, they are called *basindo nan tenggil*, which translates as "he who likes to sit high." Sun bears are great climbers who rest in trees. They sometimes make sleeping platforms out of leaves and branches many feet off the ground.

There are eight living species of bear, including polar bears, grizzly bears, and giant pandas.

A Rainbow of a Day

It's just after sunrise on the island of Nosy Be in Madagascar. The sweet smell of ylang-ylang flowers fills the air. A panther chameleon is ready to start his day. His bulging eyes search for a sunny spot to bask in. They rotate up, down, and side to side. It doesn't take long for him to find just the right spot. The chameleon ambles along toward the end of a branch in his rainforest home. The sun's rays feel delightful on his skin. And then, as if by magic, his bright blue-green body starts to darken!

After soaking in the sunshine for a while, the chameleon is nice and warm. It's time to get moving. His skin lightens and the dark stripes fade away. His pincer-like toes grip a thin branch. He takes a few steps forward. But then he slowly rocks back and forth. From a distance, he looks like a leaf swaying in the breeze. His two eyes rotate in different directions as he scans the landscape. He is looking for two things at the same time: something to eat and something that wants to eat him. For the moment, he finds neither.

Suddenly, the chameleon hears a soft **SNORING** sound. He peers into a small hollow in the trunk of the tree. Aha! A Nosy Be sportive lemur is snoozing inside. The chameleon roams on— the sleeping lemur poses no threat to him.

He climbs higher and higher. Eventually, he decides to creep out onto a branch with an ocean view. He's hard to spy among the deep green leaves. This is one of his favorite hunting spots. The chameleon keeps his body completely still. Only his eyes move. He patiently waits... and waits... and waits. Finally, one eye catches a glimpse of something delicious. It's a praying mantis sitting on a leaf. The chameleon's other eye turns and locks in on the potential meal. With lightning speed, his tongue darts out like an arrow being shot from a bow. He catches the unsuspecting mantis by the head. The mantis cannot escape its sticky grasp. The chameleon opens his mouth. **CRUNCH, GULP!**

That was tasty, but the chameleon is still hungry for more insects. Instead, he notices another panther chameleon coming closer! It starts to climb out onto his branch. The skin of our chameleon starts to change color once again. Much of his body turns a bold yellow and orange, except for a bright white line down his side. Deep red stripes with blue speckles appear, too. Royal blue stripes pop up on the rival chameleon's sides. It's a color war! The two chameleons are now nose to nose. Each tries to push the other off the branch.

They hiss loudly at each other. Our chameleon pushes again. His rival sways and loses his balance. He hangs below the branch, gripping it tightly with his toes and tail. Our chameleon uses his long tail like a whip, hitting his enemy. **WHACK!** The rival soon realizes he is not going to win this battle. His bold colors become duller and darker. He drops to a lower branch, then scurries away as fast as he can. Our chameleon has won the bright battle!

The commotion of the battle scared off any nearby insects.
The chameleon must move on if he wants to find more food.
He climbs up to the forest canopy. It pays off! He spends much
of the afternoon snagging insect after insect.

Just when he is about to head to a slightly cooler section of the tree, he hears an all-too familiar sound: **BOOP! BOOP! BOOP!** The chameleon quickly lets go of the branch, dropping several feet to another branch below. He barely escaped becoming dinner for a hungry bird called a coucal!

Scurrying away, the chameleon heads for a spot to rest for the night. What a rainbow day in the rainforest!

Masters of Color

Panther chameleons are native to Madagascar, an island off the east coast of mainland Africa. There are more than 200 species of chameleon in the world, and almost half of them live in Madagascar!

Sticky spit

A panther chameleon's tongue can stretch up to two times as long as its body. This enables it to catch prey that's a decent distance away. Its super sticky spit also helps it hunt. It can catch insects, lizards, and even small birds with ease!

Hey, little guy

Panther chameleons are some of the largest chameleons. Males can grow to be about 14–21 in (36–53 cm) long and females about 9–13 in (23–33 cm) long. The world's smallest chameleon, Brookesia nana, gets just a bit longer than 1 in (3 cm).

Unusual toes

Chameleons have two toes on one side of their foot and three toes on the other. They also have sharp claws. These features help them grasp branches easily.

The world's smallest chameleon can stand on the end of a pencil!

Color changes

Chameleons change color to show how they are feeling. If they are angry or excited, the space between tiny crystals in their skin grows larger. This causes red, yellow, or orange light to be reflected. If a chameleon is feeling calm, the space between the tiny crystals in its skin gets smaller, so green and blue light are reflected. Pretty cool, huh?

A Visit to the Baobab Tree

The afternoon sun beats down on a mother elephant and her calves in southern Africa. They are hot and thirsty as they seek out a shady spot where they can escape the blistering heat.

FLAP! FLAP! They wave their huge ears to cool off. Then they scrape the ground, grab some dry soil, and use their powerful trunks to throw it over themselves. A dust bath may not be as cooling as a wet one, but it feels good to the elephants.

The elephants set off in search of water. When they arrive at a cluster of mopane trees, the mother stops walking. Her younger calf nurses, guzzling her mother's rich milk. The older one munches some mopane leaves. Even though the leaves are dry, they taste good. While the elephants relax in the shade, a brown-headed parrot lands on a branch overhead. Its calls of **KRRA-EET** pierce the still air.

The elephants leave the shelter of the woodlands a little before sunset, continuing their search for water. In the distance, they see sable antelopes grazing on dried grasses. They pass towering sandstone cliffs, turned orange by the late afternoon sunlight.
The Runde River is barely a trickle in this dry season— certainly not enough to quench the thirst of the elephant family. So on they go.

The mother and calves roam
for two more days. They sip from
the occasional small waterhole. But
they are still so thirsty. Finally, in the
distance, the mother spots what she's been
looking for. An enormous baobab tree! The
mother makes a great TRUMPETING noise
at the sight. She walks right up to the tree and,
surprisingly, uses her tremendous tusks to poke
a hole in its bark. Then she starts to rip the
bark off the tree, one piece after another!

At first, her calves watch her every move curiously. Then they start to copy her behavior. It doesn't take long to get to the soft inside of the baobab. It's like a giant sponge, full of moisture the tree has saved. The trio of elephants happily **SLURP** it up. When they are finished, the baobab has an enormous hole in its center.

A couple of months later, the rainy season begins. Lightning strikes illuminate the sky. Showers soak the parched earth. The river is just starting to flow freely again. **SPLASH!** A baboon family make their way across it. The mother elephant and her calves feed on a variety of lush green plants. At dusk, the large white flowers of the baobab trees open. Hawk moths flutter in, sipping the flowers' sweet nectar.

The weather gets warmer and warmer. One day, while wandering with her calves, the mother elephant notices ripe baobab fruit, but it's hanging from branches way above her head. She approaches the tree and pushes its wide trunk forcefully with her tusks. Suddenly, it's raining baobab fruit! **PLONK! PLOP!** The family wastes no time. They dive into the tasty treats, swallowing both the dry white pulp and the seeds inside.

The young elephants grow and change, season after season. They forage and frolic as their mother looks on. One day, as they are roaming, they hear a tremendous **CRASH!** The baobab tree they feasted on the year before has fallen over. Mottled spinetails and red-billed buffalo weavers, who had made their homes in its upper branches, scatter in all directions.

Termites and other insects get to work devouring the remains of the once-glorious giant baobab tree. Within a year, it has completely vanished. But many other baobab trees have sprouted where the elephants left behind their seed-filled dung piles! With a little luck and help from Mother Nature, new baobab forests will grow and feed elephants and other wildlife for thousands of years to come.

The Tree of Life

The baobab tree is also known as the bottle tree. It provides shelter, food, and water for a variety of reptiles, birds, and insects. A baobab tree's trunk can store 26,000 gallons (100,000 liters) of water! This is why thirsty elephants seek out these trees during dry periods.

A worrying future

Baobab trees help keep the soil moist and prevent it from blowing away. Some of these enormous trees have lived for more than 2,000 years, but several of the oldest and largest ones in southern Africa have died in recent years. Scientists think climate change (changes in long-term weather patterns caused by humans burning oil, coal, and gas for energy) could be the cause.

Helping trees

Recently, elephants have been felling baobab trees at a worrying rate. One way to protect the trees is to surround the tree's base with big rocks. Since elephants do not like to stand on uneven surfaces, this deters them from getting too close to the trees.

Purple-crested turaco

White-backed vulture

Bird paradise

Gonarezhou National Park, where this story is set, is home to more than 400 species of bird—more than anywhere else in Zimbabwe. White-backed vultures, gray-headed parrots, and bat-like spinetails almost always build their nests in baobab trees. Other colorful flyers in the park include the green-backed twinspot, the southern carmine bee-eater, and the purple-crested turaco.

Not just for animals!

Humans can boil the baobab tree's leaves and eat them like spinach. The fruit pulp can be made into jam or juice. When roasted, baobab seeds make an alternative to coffee beans. Different parts of the tree can also be used in medicines that help fight fever and illnesses.

A Changing Home

BRUM-BRUM-BRUM-BRRRR!

A chainsaw roars into action in the central African rainforest. Streams of sawdust fill the air. Immediately, a pair of Bates's weaver birds takes flight. But these birds aren't the only animals who are startled. The chainsaw's strong vibrations also wake up a tree pangolin who'd been sleeping in a tree hollow.

The pangolin pokes its head out from its snoozing spot. It blinks in the bright sun. The revving sounds are shockingly loud— not like any animal it has ever heard before! The pangolin descends the umbrella tree and heads away from the earsplitting machine. It shuffles along the ground on its knuckles. A troop of gorillas speeds past the pangolin. They are also trying to get away from the noise.

The pangolin's body clock feels topsy-turvy. Perhaps some food will perk it up. It stands on its hind legs and sniffs, finding a termite mound nearby. **SCRATCH! RIP!** The pangolin's sharp front claws quickly tear open the nest. Thousands of termites wiggle and wriggle, trying to escape. They are no match for the pangolin's super-long, sticky tongue. It slurps down the termites, swallowing them whole. As the pangolin feasts, a tiny blue duiker wanders past. It stops not far off for its own meal of flowers.

All morning long, the pangolin moves deeper into the dense rainforest. Eventually, the sounds of the chainsaw grow quieter. The pangolin is so tired. It climbs a longhi tree to search for a new resting place. Its claws and tail give it grip and balance along the way. Once it chooses a spot, the pangolin settles down for a long nap.

The moon is high in the sky by the time the pangolin wakes up. No chainsaws buzz in the darkness. The pangolin hears a faint noise but isn't sure what the sound is. Suddenly a snake slithers past. **HISSSS**... The snake is on its way toward a bird's nest, hoping for a midnight snack.

The pangolin is thirsty so it heads out on a mission to find water. It climbs over thick tree roots and under fallen logs before reaching a small stream. Its tongue darts in and out as it laps water at lightning speed. While at the water's edge, the pangolin catches the scent of ants. It is just about to cross the stream when it glimpses something large rushing toward it.

YIKES! It's a leopard! The pangolin quickly rolls itself into a tight ball. Another few seconds, and the leopard would have had its soft belly in its jaws.

The leopard tries to bite the ball, then paws at it. For several very frustrating minutes, the big cat tries to get the ball open. It finally gives up, deciding this meal is too much work. The leopard spies a rodent, catches it, and runs off with its snack. What a lucky escape! Now that the coast is clear, the pangolin swims across the stream.

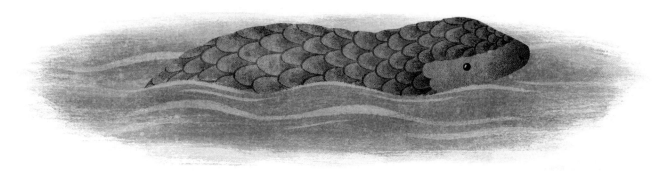

On the way back to the safety of its tree hollow, the pangolin discovers a group of stink ants in the leaf litter. But it does not notice that another tree pangolin is approaching the same feeding spot. The other pangolin is not happy. It sprays a terrible smelling liquid from its rear end. **EWW!** Our pangolin leaves the scene as fast as it can. What a stink!

Worn out by the events of the day and the night, the pangolin climbs back into its hollow before dawn. Each day, the sound of chainsaws get closer. Logging trucks come into the rainforest to collect the valuable trees that have been cut down. Within a few weeks, the pangolin is again forced to move further into the rainforest. But eventually the forest grows quiet. The pangolin delights in the natural sounds of its home—the heavy rainfall on the leaves, the birdsong that lulls it to sleep each morning, and the flowing of a stream through the Central African rainforest.

An Unusual Animal

There are eight different species of pangolin in the world. Four are found in Asia, and four live in Africa. The ones in this story live in the rainforest in Cameroon. They are tree pangolins, also known as white-bellied pangolins. Pangolins are the only mammals in the world whose bodies are covered in scales!

Tremendous tongues

The tongue of a pangolin is long and sticky. In fact, a pangolin's tongue is often longer than its whole body! This tongue allows a pangolin to lap up termites and ants with ease.

No biting!

When pangolins are feeding on ants, they have a way to protect themselves from being bitten. They can close both their ears and their nose to keep the ants out!

A single adult pangolin can eat as many as 20,000 ants in a day. That's more than 7 million insects in a year!

Swallowing stones

Because pangolins do not have teeth, they swallow the termites and ants they eat whole. They also swallow small stones and sand during their meal. These help the pangolin's stomach grind up the insects they eat.

Pangolin scales are made out of keratin—the same material that makes up your fingernails and hair.

Hitching a ride

A pangolin often gives birth to just one baby pangolin. When they're born, baby pangolins are 6 in (15 cm) long—about the size of a toothbrush! A baby pangolin's mother will stay with it and protect it until its soft scales become hard. Baby pangolins love clinging on to their mother's tail while she's walking.

Threats to pangolins

All pangolins are threatened with extinction, often because of the actions of humans. Some cultures believe that pangolin scales have medicinal value. Habitat loss is another significant threat to pangolin survival. When forests are knocked down to create roads and farms, pangolins can lose their homes.

Lost in the Forest

A fuzzy young reindeer follows his mother deep into the forest. Light snow is falling. They pass pine and spruce trees coated in a shimmering layer of ice. The mother and her calf are traveling along with their herd. They are largely quiet, except for the sounds of their feet: **CLICK! CLACK!**

The reindeer come to a clearing. Since there's only a dusting of snow on the ground, they can graze on mosses and frosty leaves. The young reindeer discovers a mushroom left over from the fall. He winds in and out of the trees, nibbling on lichens growing on their branches. He passes some antlers that must have been recently shed. Munching away, he strays farther and farther away from the herd...

It is late afternoon before the young reindeer notices he is all alone. Oh no! The sky is already starting to get dark. He wonders where the rest of the herd could have gone. He **BLEATS** and **BLEATS**, hoping his mother will hear his calls and come back to rescue him. But he is only greeted with silence. The calf heads out of the forest and into a more open area. He sniffs the air, hoping to catch the scent of his herd. Instead, he smells wood smoke from a human home in the distance.

All of a sudden, the calf feels something very sharp on the back of his neck. A golden eagle has grabbed him! It starts to fly off while the terrified reindeer flails his legs.

He calls as loudly as he can. It's enough to cause the eagle to lose its grip and drop him. Phew! That was a lucky escape. The calf dashes into the forest. The eagle chases him for a while, only giving up when it spies a brown hare in its path.

Worn out from the scary chase, the calf finds a dense stretch of evergreen trees and lies down. It is dark when he wakes up. The wind is picking up, but the reindeer's cream-colored fur keeps him warm. He starts walking into the wind, again trying to catch the scent of his herd. **SNIFF!** Though he doesn't smell his family, his furry nose helps him find food beneath the snow. He scrapes away at the snow with his hairy hooves, uncovering more tasty lichen.

For two long days and nights the scared young reindeer roams alone. He encounters a herd of elk feeding on twigs and bark in a stand of pines. The huge males stare at him, frightening the little reindeer. One night, under the swirling colors of the northern lights, he spies a lynx. Not wanting to become a midnight meal for the wild cat, the reindeer calf runs in the opposite direction as fast as his legs will take him.

After wandering for miles and miles, the young reindeer is exhausted. But still he continues to look for his mom. His eyes constantly scan the landscape for any sign of the herd. Just when it seems he'll be all alone for good, the reindeer catches a scent on the wind.

Could it be? It is! It's his herd! The calf sprints toward the smell. His mother smells him too and calls out. The calf scampers up to his mom who nuzzles him, delighted to be reunited with her baby. He'll be careful not to wander away from his herd again!

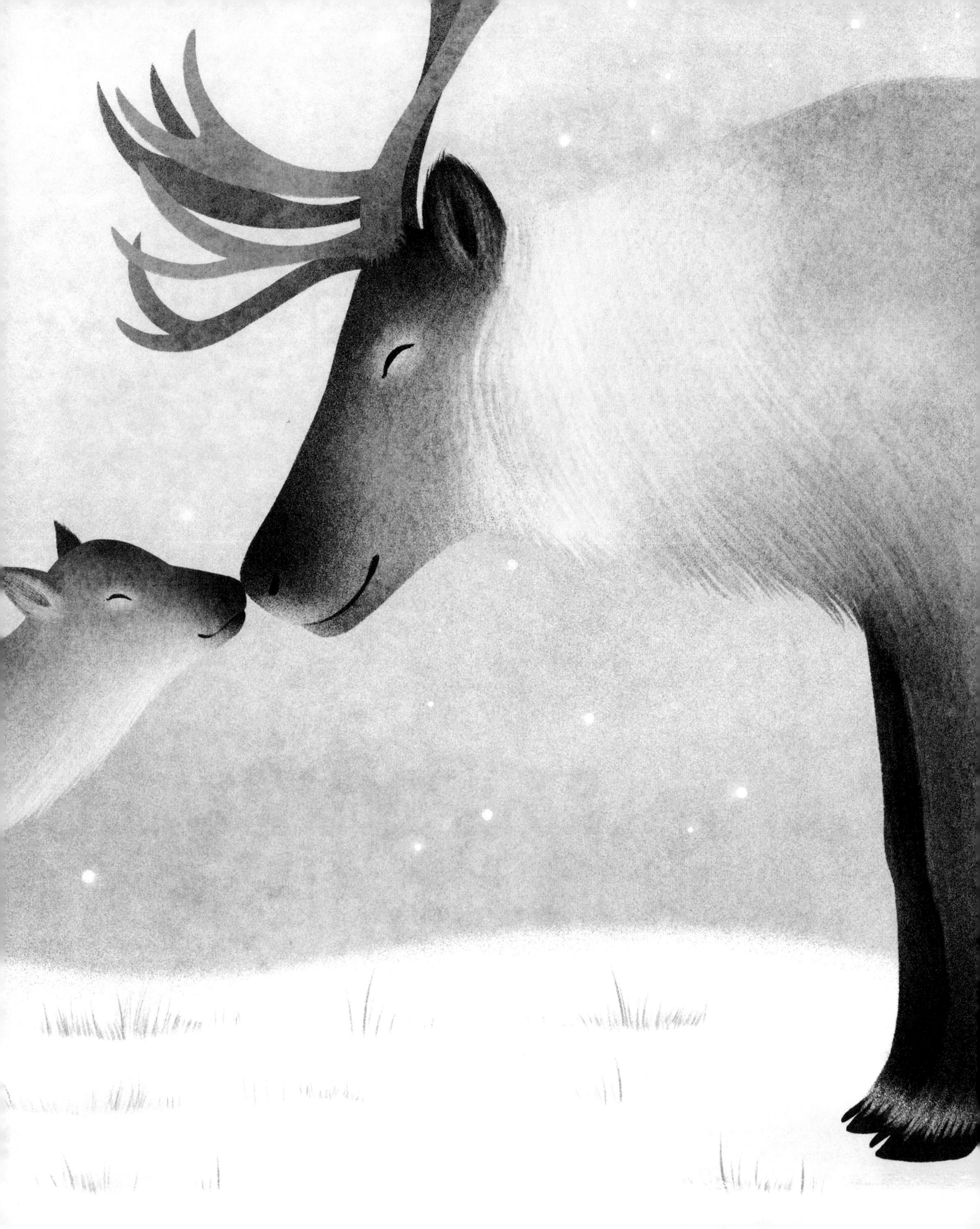

Creatures of the North

Depending on where you are in the world, reindeer go by different names. In northern Europe and Asia they're called reindeer, while in North America they're known as caribou. The reindeer herd in this story lives in Scandinavia, a region in northwest Europe.

Magnificent antlers

Both male and female reindeer have antlers. They shed and grow new ones each year. Male reindeer typically shed their antlers in November or December, while females keep theirs over the winter, shedding them in the spring. So it may be that Rudolph was actually a female reindeer!

Quick learners

Reindeer calves can stand within an hour of when they are born. By the following day they are able to move around well enough to travel with the herd. A day-old reindeer calf can run faster than a human!

Snowshoes

Reindeer have wider feet than any other type of deer. Their sharp hooves help give them grip when walking on ice. During the winter they even have hair that grows between their toes. This helps keep their hooves from getting clogged with snow.

Northern lights

Scandinavia is just one area where the northern lights, or aurora borealis, occur. These colorful lights appear in the sky at night and are best seen between September and March. They are caused by very tiny particles that have come from the sun. When these electrically charged particles enter Earth's atmosphere, they glow. They can be many different colors, including green, pink, violet, blue, and red.

Lichen lovers

Lichen is a favorite food for reindeer. Lichen is an organism made up of a combination of fungus and algae. An adult reindeer typically eats about 9–18 lb (4–8 kg) of vegetation per day. Much of this is lichen!

Playing in the Night

Something black and white is poking out from the base of a giant English oak tree. It's the twitchy snout of a badger! After **SNIFFING** to make sure the coast is clear, the badger shimmies out of its sett, or burrow. It doesn't go far. Instead, it flops down onto the soft earth between the oak and a hazel tree.

The badger rolls onto its back and starts grooming.
It scratches its belly, then its legs and tail. While it grooms,
three more badgers come out from the sett. It's the badger's
brother and sisters! They crowd in around the first one, who
rolls onto its side. The members of the badger clan begin to
groom one another. One uses its teeth to neaten up a matted
patch of fur on its sister's shoulder. Another picks out lice
and fleas from its brother's back and rump. Before long, the
badgers are ready for a night of foraging and fun!

Under the watchful eye of their mom, the young badgers head in the direction of an elder tree that they visited the night before. It stands right on the edge between their woodland home and a field. Its branches are laden with small, purple-black fruits. The cubs dive in. YUM! They scoff down the jewel-like berries until their snouts turn purple. Then they amble back toward their sett. A family of foxes who'd been watching them feast takes their place at the elder tree. It's their turn to enjoy eating the sour berries!

Back at the sett, there's work to do. The badger mom runs down one of the many underground tunnels. She quickly returns, coming out of the sett backward. Under her chin is a pile of old straw. She puts it down near one of the sett's entrance holes before gathering some dry grass, bracken, and moss from the undergrowth nearby. Carrying this collection under her chin, she shuffles backward down into her home.

One of the cubs follows her lead. He collects fallen leaves and a stick, then drags them backward into the sett. The stick may not be useful for creating a cozy sleeping space, but it's a good start for a young badger! It takes multiple trips to refresh the bedding in the sleeping chambers. While this is going on, some of the other cubs are busy pressing their rumps together. They are marking one another with scent glands under their tails.

All the hard work makes the badgers hungry for more food! They spy a huge dirt pile. Heaps of earthworms wriggle around. The badgers use their teeth to pull worm after worm from the loose soil. **SLURP!** They look like people eating pasta! After their meal, the badger cubs play. One does a somersault. Two others enjoy leapfrogging in the leaves. A game of chase gets underway. They zip past beech and silver birch trees. Some fox kits want to join in on the fun. No problem! They zigzag in the moonlight, only stopping when they come across fallen crab apples or other tasty treasures.

A bright orange light shines through the woodland. The sun is coming up! A great spotted woodpecker starts to hammer into a tree as it searches for insects. Their adventures over, it's time for the badger clan to head home. One at a time, they climb back into the hole at the base of the oak tree. Soon after, the foxes also climb into the sett. They wander through the complicated network of tunnels and chambers until they find some that are empty. Then the woodland creatures settle down to snooze the day away.

Life Underground

There are many types of badgers and foxes around the world. The ones in this story are European badgers and red foxes. They live in a forest in southern England.

Badger senses

Badgers have small eyes and cannot see very well. However, thanks to their long snout, they have an excellent sense of smell. If another animal has left its paw print on the ground, a badger can still smell it hours later. Experts say that a badger's sense of smell is about 800 times better than a human's!

Badger clans often have four to eight members, but some have as many as 20.

Smelly messages

Scent is an important part of how badgers communicate. They mark the boundaries of their territories with latrines (badger "bathrooms"). When other clans smell their poop, they steer clear to avoid conflict. Badgers also leave their scent in their territory using a scent gland under their tail. Badgers also "bum press" each other—they press this scent gland onto another member of their clan. This is so the group has a common scent.

Foxes and badgers

Foxes and badgers often live in the same areas. Both species are nocturnal, which means they are active at night. Badgers are the dominant animals. Because of this, foxes tend to give badgers their space to avoid any conflict. However, it is not uncommon for the two species to share a sett—though they would generally choose tunnels or chambers that are a fair distance from each other.

Home sweet sett

Badgers spend about 70% of their lives underground. A badger clan usually has one main sett. This sett typically includes multiple tunnels and entrances. It is also where they have their babies. A badger clan will have additional setts scattered throughout their territory, too. These can be used to rest or hide in, or by other females in the clan when they're ready to have babies.

Badger bedding

Badgers use lots of different materials as bedding in their setts. The materials vary depending on the season—from bluebells and garlic leaves in spring to dry straw later in the summer. The badgers will change all of the bedding a few times each year, typically before their cubs are born. They also take some bedding materials out into the open to air on a sunny, dry day. This helps get rid of fleas. Then, they bring the aired-out materials back into the sett!

It's early fall in southern Canada. The afternoon is sunny and warm, but the days are getting shorter. It's the sign a young monarch butterfly needs. It's almost time for this little insect to embark on an incredible journey. But first things first—it needs to stock up for the trip! The butterfly flutters its bright orange-and-black wings. It stops to sip nectar from the bright yellow blooms of a goldenrod plant. YUM! Then it flits to a coneflower to continue feeding.

An Epic Journey

The monarch's odyssey begins a few days later. In the cool early morning, it flies just above the ground. As the sun rises in the sky, the butterfly flies higher and higher. By mid-morning, the air is much warmer. The super-lightweight butterfly gets carried upward into a column of rising air called a thermal. It travels up, and up, and up... It soars over fields and winding rivers. A herd of white-tailed deer run in and out among the maple trees below. The cars driving on the highway look as small as ants.

The tiny monarch glides from one thermal to another. When evening approaches, it comes back down to the ground. It lands on a tree in Point Pelee National Park. Thousands of other monarchs are already roosting there. Suddenly, a loud **CRRR-AACK** breaks the silence of the forest. A nearby tree branch has broken from the weight of all the butterflies! Thousands of patterned wings flutter frantically in their search for another place to spend the night.

Strong winds blow through the park in the days that follow.
The butterfly stays put, safe and snug on its branch. Finally, the
skies clear and the sun shines brightly. The monarch wastes
no time. It takes off on its flight over the shimmering waters
of Lake Erie. Hundreds of other monarchs lift off as well.
They create a ribbon of orange in the sky.

For nearly two months, the young butterfly wings its way southwest. One week it flies over vast cornfields. The next it glides above sweet-smelling apple orchards. But the trip is not always smooth or easy. While basking on a warm street one morning, the butterfly is almost hit by a car! Luckily it takes flight at the last second. **GULP!** That was close.

A few days later, while flying over Missouri, terrible thunderstorms come out of nowhere. The butterfly is just getting ready to descend to roost in a bald cypress tree when enormous raindrops start to fall. A couple pelt the monarch before it can hide under the cover of some thick leaves. It takes hours before its wings are dry enough to even attempt to fly again.

At last, in early November, the monarch finally arrives at its destination! The journey, which has spanned nearly 2,500 miles (4,000 km), has taken the butterfly to the mountains of central Mexico. Here it can drink from clear streams in the humid forest. It roosts in a fir tree, while other migrating monarchs spend their nights in oak and pine trees. Even though the young butterfly spent each day flying alone, this Mexican forest is anything but solitary. Millions of monarchs—perhaps even a billion—are here to spend the winter. The trees, coated in a layer of orange, look as if they've been painted by a magical artist.

After its long journey, the butterfly looks for a mate. This tiny traveler will not return to the spot where its migration began. But, over several generations, its descendants will make it all the way back to Canada—and then back south to Mexico! If you ever see a monarch flying in the skies, wish it well for the amazing adventure that lies ahead.

Finding the way

Scientists continue to study how a monarch butterfly navigates to its wintering spot. It appears that the butterfly has a built-in compass! The compass allows it to figure out both the sun's position and what time of day it is. These pieces of information make it possible for the butterfly to head in the correct direction.

The super generation

Not all monarchs live for the same amount of time. Most live for only two to six weeks. But in the late summer, a super generation of monarch butterflies is born. These are the butterflies that make the migration from as far north as Canada down to Mexico. They can live for as long as nine months. They mate and reproduce in Mexico. It is the super generation's children, grandchildren, and so on that make the journey north. It takes three to five generations to reach the place the butterflies will spend the summer.

Monarchs on the Move

As well as North America, monarch butterflies can be found in parts of South America, Europe, Australasia, and Oceania. The one in this story lives in eastern North America.

All in a day's work

When migrating, monarchs typically fly for about 4-6 hours per day. They'll take a break in the afternoon to feed. But if the weather is too windy or rainy, they will not fly. Temperature also affects their ability to fly. Their flight muscles must be at least 55°F (13°C) to fly. That's why monarchs are often seen basking, with their wings open and tilted toward the sun. This helps them warm up so they can fly.

Record breakers

Despite their small size, monarchs migrate farther than almost any other insect. Some travel as far as 3,000 miles (4,800 km) to their wintering spot. But monarch butterflies aren't the only ones that undergo long journeys. The trophy for the longest migration out of all the animals on Earth goes to the Arctic tern. Flying from the Arctic to the Antarctic, these birds migrate around 25,000 miles (40,000 km) every year.

115

The Day the River Ran Dry

A stream rushes through the Valdivian forest, in South America, just before dusk. The water **BABBLES** and **BURBLES** as it flows over rocks and tree roots. A family of southern river otters heads toward it. It's time for the pups' nightly swimming lesson! Their mother glides gracefully into the stream and shows off her smooth moves. The pups slip and slide along the muddy streambank before plopping into the water. **SPLASH!**

The mom demonstrates her fishing skills to her pups. She catches one fish, then another, and another. She shares her food but also encourages them to try fishing themselves. One mimics her, but the wiggly fish gets away before the pup can enjoy its catch. The other pup rolls over and over in the water, splashing away and having a terrific time. It gathers a few stones and carries them onto dry land. Then the pup juggles the stones like a circus performer.

Every night, this otter family comes to the same stream. They swim, slide, and forage for food. But then one night, everything changed. The otters had just come out from their burrow beneath an olivillo tree. Instead of the rushing stream sounds, there was quiet. The river wasn't flowing anymore! The mother and her pups wandered up and down the streambed. Where was the water they used to swim in? Damp soil and dead fish were all that remained of their watery playground and pantry.

What could the otters do? They would be hungry if they stayed put. The only option was to move on. The otter pups followed closely behind their mom as she set off. They passed ulmo and tineo trees. The mother pounced quickly on a helmeted water toad—POW! The unfortunate amphibian became a late-night snack.

The pups scampered through the rainforest. One slipped on some muddy tree roots and did a somersault right into a giant puddle. **WHEEE!** A little while later, the sound of flowing water beckoned. Had they found a suitable new river? But then the otters smelled something pungent. It was fishy... or was it flowery? The mother and her pups used their noses to explore the area. Before long, they discovered where the smell was coming from—a pile of dung! That probably meant the nearby gurgling stream was another otter's territory. The mother otter wanted no trouble. She and her pups took a quick dip in the stream, caught some crabs, and kept on moving.

Later in the night, the mother stopped beneath a Chilean bellflower. The moonlight lit up its waxy green leaves and magenta flowers. She groomed her pups, combing their velvety fur with her claws. Overhead, tiny marsupials called monitos del monte ate fruit in the trees. The **TRILLING** of the "mountain monkeys" rang through the night.

Several nights passed and the otter family still hadn't found a new place to call home. Each night they scoped out places to live. Each place they visited brought new sights, smells, sounds—and adventures, of course! Once they wandered past giant alerce trees that seemed to stretch as high as the moon.

In the end, it took several nights of roaming—and sometimes running—before the mother otter found a suitable spot. It was a small river with lush trees and plants surrounding its banks. The water flowed freely and there was plenty to eat. Their mother watched the pups playing in the river. *This will do nicely*, she thought. Happy at last, the pups started to grow bigger and bigger. It didn't take long before they became skilled at catching fish, frogs, and even the occasional bird. And never again did they have to leave their home.

Super Swimmers

There are 13 otter species in the world. The ones in this story are called southern river otters and they are an endangered species. They live in the Valdivian rainforest of southern South America.

A different kind of rainforest

Most of the world's rainforests, such as the Amazon or the Congo Basin, are located in the tropics (near the equator). However the Valdivian rainforest is a temperate rainforest located outside of the tropics, in the countries of Chile and Argentina. Like all rainforests, it gets a lot of rain throughout the year. But instead of being steamy and hot, its climate is mild. The Valdivian rainforest is known for its unique plants. It has many olivillo trees, which can reach 66 ft (20 m) in height. Meanwhile its alerce trees can live to be up to 4,000 years old!

Otters share the Valdivian forest with many other animals. One of these is the pudu, the world's smallest deer.

Pudus

Where did the water go?

One of the biggest threats to southern river otters is habitat loss. When people create new farms, they often use the water from streams to build canals. These canals provide water for their crops but take away habitat and food sources from animals, such as the otters in this story.

Otters are excellent swimmers thanks to their webbed feet and strong tails.

What a smell!

Otter poop is called spraint. It's known for being particularly stinky. Some scientists describe its smell as slightly fishy, which makes sense given the amount of fish in their diet! Otters can gather information about other otters in the area from their piles of poop.

Circus performers

Otters are famous for their stone-juggling skills. Scientists have seen them juggle lying on their backs and also when standing up. Juggling stones may be a way for otters to practice their foraging skills, such as getting food out of clams or mussels. But they may also juggle when they are excited about food. Some scientists discovered that otters juggle more when they are feeling hungry!

Dancing in the Mangroves

Gentle waves lap the shore on a tropical island. The air is steamy. A family of ashy tailorbirds trill to one another. They are searching for insects in the canopy of the mangrove forest. Below them, the tide is going out. As it does, the world that had been below the water's surface starts to share its secrets.

The mudflats at the edge of the mangroves become more and more visible. Soon, the tangled roots of a mangrove tree come into view. Once the waters have receded far enough away from the shore, a fish called a blue-spotted mudskipper emerges. He slowly hauls himself out from his burrow beneath the mud. His fins give him the final push he needs to plop onto the mudflats' gloopy surface. **SPLAT!**

Before he moves anywhere, the mudskipper looks to see who else is around. Loads of other mudskippers are scattered around. Some are blue-spotted ones like him. Others are smaller dusky-gilled mudskippers. He spots a giant mudskipper building a pool in the distance.

Today's a big day for our mudskipper. He'll need a lot of energy for the task that lies ahead. He starts by rolling over and over again, coating himself in mud. Next, he moves his wide head quickly from side to side. He's combing the muddy surface in order to find food. Then he notices some small crabs not far away.

Just then, the mudskipper does something very un-fishlike. Using his fins to propel him forward, he starts to walk over the mud! **FLAP! DRAP! FLAP! DRAP!** He squelches all the way across the mudflat. Eventually, he catches up to a small crab. Chomp! Into his mouth it goes.

With a hearty meal in his belly, the mudskipper rolls in the mud a few more times to keep himself damp. Now it's time to put on a show. Many female mudskippers are on the mudflat. They are all waiting to choose a mate. But our mudskipper has competition. He's not the only male trying to impress the ladies, so he's going to have to do something spectacular.

Before he gets a chance to impress, another male mudskipper approaches. He sees our mudskipper as a rival. A battle of the big mouths ensues! Each mudskipper opens its mouth. Their dorsal fins stand straight up. Then they lunge at each other. They make gurgling and popping sounds as they fight. **GHRRRL! POP! PLOFT!** A couple of minutes later, our mudskipper wins the battle. The loser moves on to another section of the mudflat.

After one last quick roll in the mud, the mudskipper is finally ready. He starts to dance! He leaps as high as he can into the air, flaring his fins. Over and over, he wiggles and waggles above the mudflat. Oozy mud splatters every time he lands. Soon his jazzy jumping catches the attention of a female mudskipper.

As the female follows the male to his cozy burrow, the delightful scent of mangrove tree flowers fills the air. The female lays her eggs, then she leaves to find food. Day after day, the tides come in and go out. The female swims and splashes around. But the male is busy with dad duties. He swims to the water's surface and takes a big gulp of air. HUFF! Then he swims back down and exhales the air into the burrow he built. PUFF! Up and down. Up and down. Up and down. Over and over, he fills the chamber with air.

The mudskipper pays close attention to the tides and the time. After about a week, he decides the moment is right. He returns to his burrow of eggs. But this time, instead of adding air, he gulps it from inside the burrow and blows it out. Water floods into the burrow. This gives a signal to the babies that it's time to hatch! The little mudskippers swim up, up, up and away, ready to begin their own adventures in the mangroves.

The Walking Fish

More than 30 different species of mudskippers live around the globe. They live in mangroves, coastal mudflats, and estuaries. The blue-spotted mudskippers in this story live in the mangrove forests of Singapore, in Southeast Asia.

Swimming pool

The giant mudskipper found in Singapore's mangroves and mudflats has a distinctive black stripe along its side. When the tide is low, it can build its own swimming pool! It digs into the mud and spits it out to form the pool. This keeps a layer of water around the mudskipper's body so it stays moist even when the tide is out.

Eye see you!

A mudskipper's eyes are located close together at the top of its head. From this vantage point, a mudskipper has an almost 360° view of what's around it. Each eye can move independently of the other. This means that mudskippers can see both below and above the water at the same time! When these fish are out of water, their eyes appear to sink into their heads. What's actually happening? Their eyes retract into a special cup filled with fluid so they stay moist.

Dazzling dancers

In the muddy environment in which mudskippers live, it can be challenging to stand out when looking for a mate. Male mudskippers put on quite a display to catch the attention of females. Their pectoral fins are both stiff and strong and give them the push to get in the air. They leap and flaunt their fins, launching themselves more than 1½ ft (0.5 m) above the ground!

The dusky-gilled mudskipper can climb trees because of its flexible fins.

Tricks up its sleeve

Mudskippers are famous for their ability to walk. Their strong front fins propel them across a mudflat. The way they move is sometimes described as "crutching," since they look like a person walking using crutches. It's common for mudskippers to perch on rocks or mangrove roots at high tide. But some mudskippers, like the dusky-gilled mudskipper, are even able to climb trees!

What the **Kauri** Tree has Seen

A long, long time ago—more than a thousand years ago— in New Zealand, a brown, winged seed traveled on the wind. It **FLITTERED** and **FLUTTERED**, past trees, orchids, and ferns of brilliant green on its way to the bottom of a kauri forest. Without a sound, the seed landed. Other seeds, twigs, leaves, and deep brown pine cones had cushioned its fall.

The seed took root in the weathered soil and started to grow. Its long, bronze leaves stood out against the kauri grass nearby. Sometimes kākāpō birds fed on leaves in the trees above. Other times they rolled up balls of moss on the forest floor. Year in and year out, the kauri seedling grew. But the process was slow, just like the movement of kauri snails crawling across the ground.

When it was young, the kauri tree looked like most other conifer trees. Bright green leaves spiraled out from its short branches. Its crown was narrow and shaped like a triangle. But as the seasons changed, so did the kauri tree. Its trunk grew a little wider year after year.

Every spring, shining cuckoos laid their eggs in the nests of gray warblers, leaving the warblers to care for their chicks. But months later, the young cuckoos would leave the kauri forest for warmer islands.

After a few decades, the kauri tree started to shed its lower branches. Its uppermost branches spread out into a beautiful crown. New seedlings sprouted far below, just like our kauri did years ago.

Hundreds of years passed. With its thick trunk and its dense canopy, the kauri tree had become a king of the forest.

One year, a group of Māori, the Indigenous people of New Zealand, cut down a kauri tree growing nearby and turned it into a beautifully carved canoe. Throughout the centuries, more often than not, the Māori left the kauri trees to stand tall. They also collected kauri tree gum. Sometimes they soaked the gum in water, mixed it with plant milk, and chewed it like bubble gum. Other times, they combined it with animal fat. They used this to decorate themselves with richly patterned tattoos.

Things changed in the late 1700s when European ships arrived. Saws and the loud thuds of kauris hitting the ground replaced the sounds of the once peaceful forest. **BRUM BRUM-BRRRR! THUD! THUD!** Sacred kingfishers and fantails fled as tree after tree was felled and taken away. Our kauri tree was deep enough in the forest to be spared. Many other trees in the area that had been growing for centuries were not so fortunate.

Hundreds of years later, people started replanting kauris and protecting them from harm. During the day, people came to the kauri forest with binoculars and cameras instead of axes and saws. Children visited our kauri tree with their parents and grandparents. They marveled at its majesty. At night, the loud whistles of brown kiwi birds filled the forest, just as they had when the kauri tree was a seedling more than a thousand years earlier.

Ancient Giants

Kauri trees have been around since the days when dinosaurs roamed the Earth. Today there are about 20 different species in locations from Australia to Fiji to Malaysia. The ones in this story are New Zealand kauri trees growing on the North Island of New Zealand.

Life cycle

Kauri trees are conifers, or cone-bearing trees. Both male and female cones grow on a kauri tree. The male cones are shaped like a finger and turn dark brown as they ripen. The male cone releases pollen, which fertilizes the round female cone, causing seeds to form. The wind disperses these winged seeds, leading to the growth of new kauri trees.

On average, a kauri tree grows about 1.2 ft (0.36 м) in height a year.

Floating wood

Because kauri wood floats, the Māori carved some kauri trees into canoes known as waka. A famous waka named *Ngātokimatawhaorua* is the world's biggest one still in use. It was made from three huge kauri trees and is 115 ft (35 m) long.

The Lord of the Forest

New Zealand is home to a number of amazingly large kauri trees. The biggest in the country is Tāne Mahuta, often known as "The Lord of the Forest." Scientists estimate that this tree is about 2,000 years old. Tāne Mahuta is as tall as a 12-story building! It grows in the Waipoua Forest, which is protected by the New Zealand government.

Deforestation

When the first European ships came to New Zealand in the late 1700s, kauri trees were abundant. They grew from the Kaimai Range to the far northern stretches of the North Island, covering nearly 3 million acres. But sadly, most of the kauri forest had been chopped down by 1900.

The Bird
Who Liked
to Build

It was a hot, sunny day in the Australian rainforest. A tree kangaroo napped on a branch high up in the canopy. On the ground below, an artist was hard at work. But this clever creator was not a person. It was a male satin bowerbird!

This was no ordinary construction project. The bowerbird was building a bower to impress a mate! He gathered small twigs from the forest floor. Then he wove in dried grass stems from a nearby field. The two walls of his bower were tall and curved with a lane in between them. The bowerbird hopped all around his bower. He flew above it. It was the right shape for sure!

He perched on a giant red cedar tree to check it out from a distance. His bower was nice. But something was missing. What was it? The bowerbird racked his brain. Still, he was stumped.

The bowerbird took to the skies. It wasn't long before he spied another bird's bower. He winged his way down to get a closer look. The shape was just like his. But then he noticed something. It was covered in paint! That was what was missing. He quickly collected some pine needles and brought them back to his construction zone. He chewed them up, mixing them with spit. He spread the gooey brown paste on the inside walls of the bower. **VOILA!** His masterpiece was finished.

Days and days went by, but no female birds came to look at his creation. Something was still missing… Again, the bowerbird took flight high above the rainforest.

Suddenly, he saw a flash of yellow. He swooped down to get a closer look. It was a golden bowerbird! He was covering his bower with white berries, flowers, and greenish-gray moss. That was it! His bower needed some decorations.

Did he want white decorations for his bower? No, that was too boring. His sharp eyes scanned the rainforest for just the right color. Something shiny and green caught his eye. It was a stag beetle crawling on a leaf. Was it beautiful? Yes! Was it the color he wanted? No. So he moved along.

Next he noticed a red straw on the ground. Was it beautiful? Yes! Was it the color he wanted? No. So he moved along.

Then, just as he was about to give up, he came upon a wondrous sight. Dozens of blue quandong berries lay scattered on the ground. Bright blue! That was the color he'd been looking for all along. Some of the berries had been nibbled by spectacled flying foxes. Others were chomped by large flightless birds called cassowaries. But there were still some left for the bowerbird. He put a couple in his beak and headed home.

The next day, the bowerbird was excited. His eyes searched high and low for more blue things. His first treasure of the day was a brilliant blue parrot feather. A pen cap was next, followed by a blue hair tie and a plastic peg. From sunrise to sunset, the bowerbird flitted about finding all sorts of gems for his bower. He was absolutely thrilled with the royal blue milk bottle cap and the shiny indigo foil candy packaging. He carefully arranged and rearranged all of the blue objects around the bower until he was satisfied.

The next morning, the bowerbird preened his feathers. He wanted to look his best. His blue-black feathers shone in the sunlight. Suddenly, a female satin bowerbird entered the bower. She peered out from the painted twigs. The bowerbird held up his best blue bottlecap to show her. **CHATTER! HISS! BUZZ! RATTLE!** He sang his heart out for his admirer. He flicked his wings and pumped his tail. He even did a pirouette. The female was impressed! The bowerbird's happy songs echoed through the rainforest, bringing joy to all who heard them.

An artist

Some male bowerbirds paint the walls of their bowers. Materials used for color include charcoal dust, plant juices, fruits, and chewed leaves, which are often mixed with spit. Some birds paint using their beaks. Others use chewed-up bark like a paintbrush!

An Industrious Bird

Satin bowerbirds are just one of the roughly 20 types of bowerbirds on Earth. All bowerbirds live in Australia and New Guinea, with satin bowerbirds dwelling in eastern Australia.

Favorite colors

Different bowerbirds prefer different colors. Satin bowerbirds decorate their bowers with blue objects. Great bowerbirds like white and gray items, dotted with red, purple, and green pieces. Striped gardener bowerbirds are fond of yellow, red, and blue objects. Meanwhile, the spotted bowerbird likes white, silver, and pink items.

Spotted bowerbird

Great bowerbird

Blue bandits

Male satin bowerbirds often steal blue objects from each other! Tail feathers are the most commonly stolen treasures. And the most popular objects on display? Plastic bottle tops with a dark blue plastic lining.

Boogie time

To impress a female, a bowerbird can't rely on its bower alone. Spectacular dancing can help convince a female he is a suitable mate. And if you've got some funky feathers, why not show them off?

Flame bowerbird

155

Glossary

Amphibian
A cold-blooded animal that breathes through gills and lives in the water when it is young, but breathes through its skin and lungs and can live on land as an adult. Toads, frogs, salamanders, and newts are amphibians.

Arboreal
Something that lives in or spends time in trees.

Basking
Lying in the sun or sunbathing. Some animals (especially cold-blooded ones) do this to control their body temperature.

Biodiversity
The variety of life forms (such as plants and animals) in an environment or ecosystem.

Burrow
A tunnel or hole in the ground made by an animal (such as a badger) where it can live or seek shelter.

Cache
A hidden place where food items are stored. Squirrels, for example, store acorns under the ground in caches.

Camouflage
The natural form or coloring of an animal that allows it to blend in with its habitat or surroundings.

Canopy
The uppermost layer of a forest. It is made up of branches and leaves that spread out at the tops of trees.

Colony
A community of one kind of animal or plant that live close together. Seals and penguins are two types of animals that live in colonies.

Crèche
A group of young animals (such as penguins) that gather in one place to be protected and cared for.

Crustacean
A member of the water-dwelling group of animals that typically have a hard covering (exoskeleton). Examples include shrimp, crabs, and lobsters.

Deforestation
The process of clearing or cutting down forests.

Den
The resting place or shelter of a wild animal. Dens are often built underground, but they can also be made in snow or inside a cave. Many animals, from rabbits to bears to foxes, have dens.

Ecosystem
A community where living things such as plants and animals interact with nonliving things such as air, water, and soil.

Endangered species
Species that are at risk of dying out (becoming extinct).

Extinction
When a group of living animals or plants no longer exist.

Foraging
Wandering about in search of things to eat.

Habitat
The place or environment where where a plant or animal spends most of its time.

Herd
A big group of animals, such as reindeer, that live, feed, and/or migrate together.

Hibernation
Spending the winter in a resting or dormant state to save energy.

Migration
The seasonal process where animals move from one region to another for breeding or feeding.

Native
Living or growing naturally in a particular place.

Nectar
A sugary liquid produced by plants, often inside flowers, to encourage insects and other animals to pollinate them. Bees also collect nectar to make honey.

Nocturnal
An animal that is active at night.

Omnivore
An animal that eats both plants and animals.

Predator
An animal that catches, kills, and eats other animals.

Prey
An animal that is caught, killed, and eaten by another animal.

Scent gland
An organ in an animal's body that secretes a smelly substance. This substance can be used to attract a mate or scare off a predator.

Seedling
A young plant or tree.

Sett
The burrow or den of a badger.

Thawing
Going from a frozen to a soft or liquid state as a result of warming.

Index

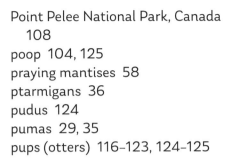

This has been a

NEON ⬡ SQUID

production

To Pete, who always encourages me to explore my curiosity whether through writing projects, travel, or trying to find out what every fungi in our local forest is. May our adventures continue and may you find many more really big trees along the way...

Author: Alicia Klepeis
Illustrator: Kristen Adam
Consultant: Dr. Brittney G. Borowiec

Editorial Assistant: Malu Rocha
US Editor: Allison Singer Kushnir
Proofreader: Joseph Barnes
Indexer: Elizabeth Wise

Copyright © 2023 St. Martin's Press
120 Broadway, New York, NY 10271

Created for St. Martin's Press
by Neon Squid
The Stables, 4 Crinan Street,
London, N1 9XW

EU representative: Macmillan
Publishers Ireland Ltd,
1st Floor, The Liffey Trust Centre,
117–126 Sheriff Street Upper, Dublin
1, D01 YC43

10 9 8 7 6 5 4 3 2 1

Library of Congress Cataloging-in-Publication Data is available.

Printed and bound in Guangdong, China by Leo Paper Products Ltd.

ISBN: 978-1-684-49311-1

Published in October 2023.

www.neonsquidbooks.com